ANNIE and SIMON

ANNIE and SIMON

Catharine O'Neill

CANDLEWICK PRESS
CAMBRIDGE, MASSACHUSETTS

To Julian, Sam, and Jarrah

First edition 2008

Library of Congress Cataloging-in-Publication Data

O'Neill, Catharine.
Annie and Simon / Catharine O'Neill. — 1st ed.
p.   cm.
Summary: Recounts four adventures of Annie,
her big brother, Simon, and their dog, Hazel.
ISBN 978-0-7636-2688-4
[1. Brothers and sisters — Fiction. 2. Dogs — Fiction.]   I. Title.
PZ7.O5524Ann 2007
[E] — dc22   2006047521

2 4 6 8 10 9 7 5 3 1

Printed in China

This book was typeset in Berkeley
with hand lettering by the author-illustrator.
The illustrations were done in watercolor.

Candlewick Press
2067 Massachusetts Avenue
Cambridge, Massachusetts 02140

visit us at www.candlewick.com

Contents

CHAPTER ONE

The Hairdo 1

CHAPTER TWO

The Loon Hunt 15

CHAPTER THREE

The Bee Sting 31

CHAPTER FOUR

The Falling Star 45

CHAPTER ONE
The Hairdo

Annie tickled Simon's foot with her green comb.

"Yoo-hoo, big brother! Guess what I've been doing?"

Simon looked up. "What, Annie?"

"Fixing Hazel's hair," said Annie. "When I grow up, I'm going to be a hairdresser."

Simon looked at Hazel. Then he turned a page. "There's an idea," he said.

Annie looked at Simon's head. "Can I fix your hair, Simon?"

"My hair?" said Simon.

"Hazel hardly has any," said Annie.

Simon stopped reading and sat up. "My hair doesn't need fixing, Annie."

"It does, too, Simon. Hold still."

Annie combed the hair on top of Simon's head straight up.

She combed the sides straight out.

She patted the back down flat.

3

"There," she said. "Now you look pretty."

Annie held up a mirror and showed Simon his new hairdo.

"Holy cow!" said Simon.

"Now let's play cards," said Annie.

Annie laid out the cards. "My turn," she said.

Annie picked up two cards and put them back.

Hazel jumped up and licked Simon's hairdo.

"Hazel, lie down," said Simon. Hazel didn't.

Simon picked up two cards and two cards and two cards.

"She'll listen to me, Simon. Hazel, LIE DOWN!" said Annie.

But Hazel didn't.

"Hey, I won!" said Simon.

"Let's not play cards," said Annie.

"You know, Annie," said Simon, "if you're going to be a hairdresser, maybe you should give yourself a new hairdo."

Simon went back to reading his book.

Annie picked up the comb. She combed her hair up and down and all around.

"Hey, this is fun," she said.

Soon Annie's hair was all done. And it wouldn't come undone.

"Eeeeeek!" said Annie.

Hazel leaped and barked at Annie's hairdo.

"HAZEL, LIE DOWN!" said Annie.

But Hazel didn't.

"What's up?" asked Simon. He came over to have a look. "Annie, what have you done?"

Annie pulled her sweater over her head. "I wound up my hair and it's all stuck."

"Let me see," said Simon.

Annie took the sweater off her head.

"Lord love a duck," said Simon. "It really is stuck."

Simon twisted Annie's comb a little this way and a little that.

"Ouch!" said Annie. "Maybe I won't be a hairdresser, Simon. I could be . . . a baker."

"Huh," said Simon. "There's an idea."

"Can I have a cookie, Simon?"

Simon found a pair of scissors.

"Hold still, Annie. I'll cut the comb to bits."

"Aaaaaagh!" said Annie.

One by one, Simon snipped off each tooth of Annie's comb. He wiggled the comb a little this way and a little that. Then he pulled the comb from Annie's hair.

"There," said Simon. "Now you have your old hairdo back."

Annie held up the mirror to see.

Then she tapped Simon's head. "Simon, Simon, look! Hazel's lying down!"

"At last," said Simon. "Here, Annie. Have another cookie."

Annie and Simon munched on their cookies.

"You know what, Simon?"

"What?"

Annie scratched Hazel's tummy. "When I grow up, I'm going to be a dog trainer."

Simon took a bite of his cookie. "There's an idea," he said.

CHAPTER TWO
The Loon Hunt

It was a noisy day at Pickerel Lake.

Annie sat in the canoe and ate blueberries.

"Want one, Simon?"

"Yup," said Simon. "No barking, Hazel."

"I think Hazel heard something," said Annie.
"I think I heard it, too. I think it was a loon."

Simon popped a blueberry into his mouth.
"All I hear is barking," he said.

Annie climbed out of the blue canoe. "Hey, Simon," she said. "Let's go on a loon hunt."

"A loon hunt!" said Simon. "Well . . . OK. But no jumping around, Annie. The canoe is tippy."

"Oh, I won't jump around," said Annie.

Simon raised one eyebrow.

Annie helped Hazel into the canoe. Simon raised his other eyebrow.

"Don't worry, Simon. Hazel won't bark."

Simon helped Annie into the front of the
canoe. Simon climbed into the back. Hazel sat in
between.

"I'm paddling, too," said Annie.

"Uh-oh," said Simon, and off they went.

The blue canoe wobbled around the point. Simon stopped paddling. "Look, Annie! Turtles."

"Turtles! But we have to find the loon, Simon." Annie plunked her paddle up and down. Hazel barked. One by one, the turtles slid into Pickerel Lake.

"Annie," said Simon, "you're getting me all wet."

"That's all right, Simon. Loons don't mind if you're wet."

The canoe splashed into the marsh. Simon
smiled. "Look, Annie! Water lilies."

Annie leaned over the side of the canoe and
pulled on a stem. "You know what, Simon?
Loons eat water lilies!"

"No, they don't," said Simon. "They eat fish—
and if you don't sit right in the middle, Annie,
we're going to fall in."

Annie stopped pulling. "Simon, I think I hear something."

Simon looked around. "All I hear is barking."

"Hazel's talking to the loon, Simon. Maybe I could talk to the loon, too."

"Soon I'll be talking to the loon," said Simon. "Look, a muskrat."

Annie sat up straight and tilted her head. "This is my loon call, Simon. Uh–ha–ha–ha–ha–ha–ha–ha–ha . . . uh–ho–ho–ho–ho–ho–ho–ho–ho!"

"That was pretty loony," said Simon. "Look, Annie! A heron."

"But where's the loon, Simon? I want to find the loon."

"We'll find the loon. Now try to sit more in the middle, Annie."

"I AM sitting in the middle, Simon."

Simon spotted something in a bush by the
water. "Look, Annie! An old nest."

"I like nests, Simon."

"Hang on. I'll get it for you."

Gingerly, Simon stood up and reached out.

"The loon didn't answer my call," said Annie.
"Do you think it's underwater?" Annie leaned out
to see.

"Look, Annie! There's a—" The blue canoe wobbled and shook. "HEY!" yelled Simon.

The blue canoe tipped Annie and Simon and Hazel into Pickerel Lake.

Annie floated around. She looked at the sky.
"The canoe IS tippy, Simon."

"I believe it is," said Simon. He waded over
to Annie.

"Here's your nest, Annie."

"Thank you, Simon."

Simon swung Annie and Hazel up into the canoe. "Let's go back now, Annie. I'm cold. No loons today."

"No loons today yet," said Annie.

Simon pulled the canoe onto the shore. Annie and Hazel clambered out.

"That was a good loon hunt," said Simon. "There were lots of wild animals."

"Oh, yes," said Annie. "Lots of wild animals."

Hazel ran around in circles. "But I'm still waiting for the loon, Simon."

Annie and Simon snuggled up in their towels.

"Want a blueberry, Simon?"

"Shhh, Annie. Hazel's asleep." Simon popped the blueberry into his mouth. "Quiet at last."

"I don't think so," whispered Annie. "Look!"

Simon raised both eyebrows at once. "How about that!" he said. "The loon."

CHAPTER THREE
The Bee Sting

Hazel was resting in her little house.

Annie sat nearby and twirled her red and white umbrella. "Do you think it's going to rain, Simon?"

Annie's big brother stopped reading. He looked up at the sky. "Nope," he said.

Annie patted Hazel's nose.

"Dogs know when it's going to rain," she said. "Hazel looks nervous."

Simon got up and peeked at Hazel. "She looks fine to me, Annie."

"Well, you do never know," said Annie. "Maybe the wind will blow the clouds here, Simon, and the rain will fall out of the clouds. And then I'll be ready with my umbrella."

"Hmm," said Simon.

Simon sat down on the steps.

Annie and Hazel stood outside under the umbrella and waited for rain.

"Simon, I hear the wind," called Annie.

"I don't hear anything, Annie," Simon called back.

"It's just a little, quiet wind, Simon."

Annie held out her hand.

"Simon, I felt a raindrop," called Annie.

"There aren't even any clouds," Simon called back.

"It was just a tiny, not-very-wet raindrop, Simon."

Hazel got tired of waiting for rain.

Annie got tired, too. "Want to pick flowers, Simon?"

"I'm reading my book, Annie."

Hazel barked and barked.

"Good grief. What's that racket, Annie?"

"Hazel's found a bug, Simon. Come see."

Simon came to see.

"There it is," said Annie, and she gave Hazel's bug a wee poke with her finger.

"Hey!" cried Annie. "It bit me." Annie dropped her flowers and the red and white umbrella. She held up her finger and ran as fast as she could to the house.

Simon ran too. "I think it was a bee, Annie."

"A bee?" cried Annie. "I got bitten by a bee!"

Annie crawled into Hazel's little house and pulled the door shut.

Simon crouched down. "Poor Annie. Can I see?"

Annie didn't answer. She held her finger tight.

"Just stick your finger out a little bit, Annie," said Simon.

Annie stuck her finger out a little bit.

"Aha," said Simon. "Hold on."

Simon got a box of baking soda and a cup of water from the kitchen. He made a little paste.

"Here, Annie. This will help."

Annie let Simon dab some paste on the sore spot.

"My first bee sting," said Annie. She held up her finger. Everyone had a good look.

"Does it hurt much?" asked Simon.

"Yes," said Annie.

Simon gave Annie a ride outside.

Annie picked up her flowers and her umbrella. She looked at the sky. "No clouds yet, Simon."

"True," said Simon. "Still, I'd hang on to your umbrella."

"You would, Simon? Do you really think it's going to rain?"

Simon didn't answer. He fiddled with something next to the steps.

Annie looked at the sky again. She held out her hand. "Hey!" she yelled. "I feel lots and lots of raindrops."

Annie and Hazel sat on the steps under the red and white umbrella.

"You do never know," said Simon.

CHAPTER FOUR
The Falling Star

Annie spread a newspaper on the kitchen floor.
Then she took down the big bowl and lots of
good things from the shelves.

"What's up, Annie?" asked Simon. He played a
loud, low note on his guitar.

"Hazel and I are making a special drink,
Simon. Want some?"

Simon got down on his hands and knees and peeked into the bowl. "Uh, no thanks," he said.

But something caught Simon's eye. "Hey, Annie, look! The newspaper says there'll be meteor showers tonight."

"What's that?" asked Annie.

Simon wiggled his fingers. "Lots of stars fall out of the sky," he said.

"Ooh. That sounds messy," said Annie. She emptied a bottle into the bowl.

"Well, they sort of fall from one side of the sky to the other," said Simon. "We could watch them from the park."

"Oh boy!" said Annie. "Can we stay up late? Can I bring my backpack? Can Hazel come?"

"Yes. Yes. No," said Simon. "Hazel barks too much."

Simon rolled up a pillow in a blanket. Hazel wagged her tail.

"Well, all right," said Simon.

When twilight came, everyone set out for the park.

"Guess what," said Annie. "I put the special drink in my backpack."

"You did?" said Simon.

"Yes," said Annie. "I'm thirsty. Let's have some now."

"Let's walk to the park first, Annie."

Annie and Hazel followed Simon to the park. Then everyone climbed to the top of the hill.

"This is a nice spot, Simon. Look at the sky. . . . Look at the colors. . . . Is it late yet?"

Simon spread out their blanket.

"It's nearly late," said Simon. "It'll be dark soon. Then we'll see the falling stars."

Annie took off her backpack. "Oh boy," she said. "Now let's have my special drink."

Annie and Simon sat on the blanket.

Annie held out two cups, and Simon poured the special drink. He took a sip. "What's in it, Annie?"

"Ginger ale, orange juice, cocoa powder, and maple syrup."

"Aaaagh! I've been poisoned," said Simon. He stuck out his tongue.

"You have not!" said Annie. She put down her cup and hunched her shoulders.

"I'm not going to be your little sister anymore, Simon."

Annie stuck her head in the backpack.

Simon gazed at the sky. "Hey, Annie, guess what."

"I'm not talking to you, Simon. What?"

"It's almost dark," said Simon.

"I'm not listening," said Annie.

"And kind of starry," said Simon.

Suddenly he pointed at the sky.

"Annie!" said Simon. "There's one!"

Annie looked out from under her backpack. "Where?" she asked.

"Over there!" said Simon. He waved his arm around. "And look, Annie! There's one! And there's one!"

"Where? Where?" asked Annie. "I never see them. I always miss them."

Annie began to cry.

"Don't cry, little sister," said Simon.

"I'm not your little sister anymore. Remember?"

"Gosh, I forgot," said Simon. "Hey, Annie. Let's have a sip of your special drink."

"We can't," said Annie. "Hazel drank it all up."

Annie rubbed her eyes. She patted Hazel's soft
rump. Then she tugged on Simon's shirt.

"Simon!" she yelled. "I saw a falling star!"

"Where, Annie?"

"You missed it, Simon. It was beautiful."

Annie and Simon and Hazel put their heads
together.

"This is my favorite night of all my life, Simon."

"It's great," said Simon. "Only one thing . . ."

"What?" asked Annie.

"I wish I had my little sister back again."

"Oh, Simon," said Annie. "I'm already your little sister back again."

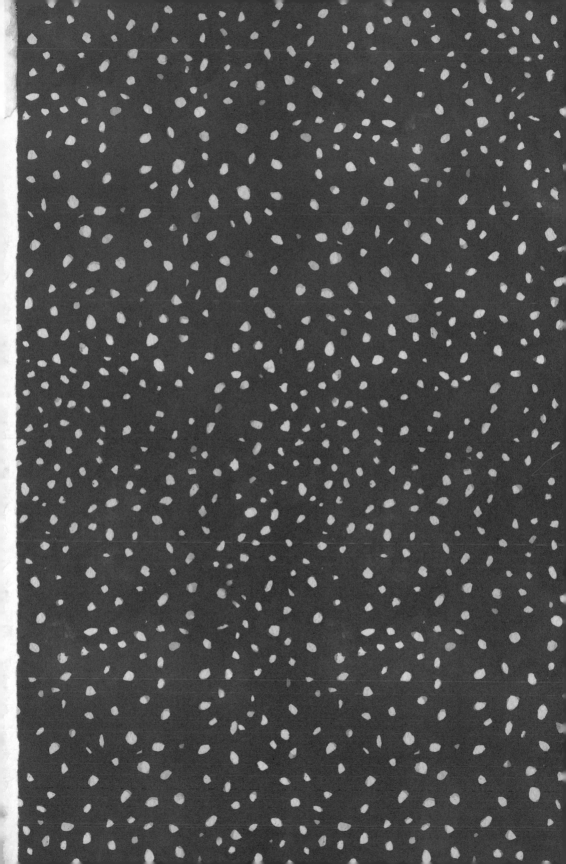

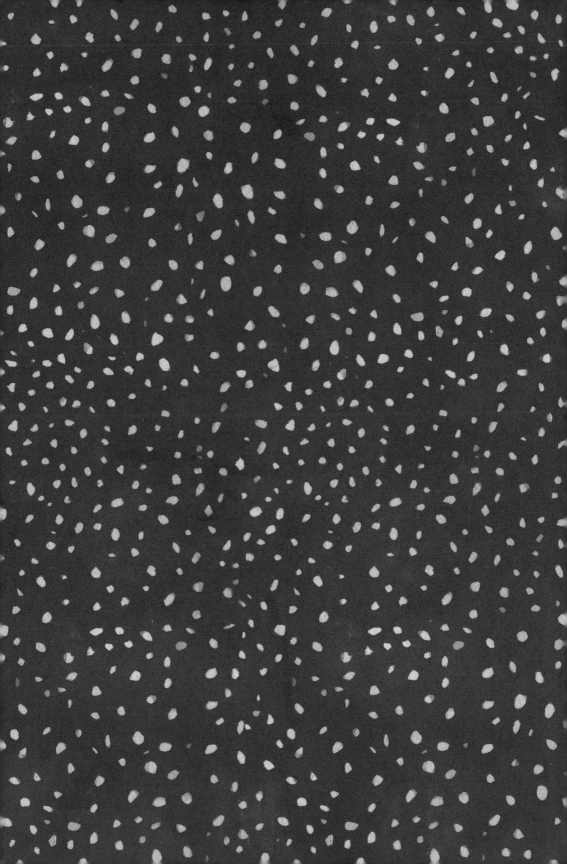